The Buzzard and The Bikers

Valerie Belsey

Illustrations by Amoria Horning

ELSP

First published in 2017 by
ELSP

www.ex-librisbooks.co.uk

Origination by Ex Libris Press

Cover photographs by courtesy of Chris Grady Photographers
Combe Raleigh, Devon

Printed by TPM Ltd.,
Farrington Gurney, Somerset

ISBN 978-1912020-64-5

© 2017 Valerie Belsey (text)
©2017 Amoria Horning (illustrations)

All enquiries and correspondence regarding this
book and the author's books on Green Lanes
should be addressed to:
valeriebelsey@gmail.com

*For all those who have known what it is like to fly, free as a bird, on a bicycle,
especially my Mum and Dad*

CONTENTS

1	Mired in the Gloop	5
2	Cousins at Crossways	13
3	Skydiving	24
4	*Buteo buteo* and the beast	38
5	Dirt Jumpers and Rooties	49
6	*'Fourpence for a Busarde'* – Henry VIII's blood money	60
7	The Hut in the Woods	71
8	Slamming on the Binders	84
9	Roaring Risers	94
10	All go for Green	101

1 MIRED IN THE GLOOP

As soon as Charlie stepped into the slithery farmyard he knew it wouldn't be long before he was mired in the gloop.

A slime of rain covered the yard of Crossways Farm. It was fine drizzle now but could easily turn to constant stinging lashes blown in by the dark grey clouds bulking up overhead. The earth would churn up like Christmas pudding mix in no time.

'Perfect, perfect,' he shouted as he slid across the yard to where his thumper lay waiting in its own stable.

There it stood, its bright orange and yellow paintwork, lighting up the dingy stable walls. He flicked up the kick stand, one of the first additions he had made, and grabbed hold of the handlebars. He pressed down gently testing the bouncy resistance of this wonderful machine. This was the trial bike that Charlie had spent a long time converting into an Enduro. He had swapped the nineteen-inch rear wheel for an eighteen-incher using Talon hub and Excel

rims. The rock hard suspension had been stripped away and replaced with one of the plushiest cross-country set-ups money could buy. As he wheeled it free from the stable the bounce in the forks over the cobbles kicked back and made him whoop with glee. Charlie did a lot of whooping. Charlie was a noisy boy. His voice was loud and his footsteps big and stumpy. You always knew when Charlie was around. When he did anything there was a lot of noise and tools got slapped down, things were knocked over. He did everything with a big voice and a big smile.

He had first fitted his trial bike out with a hefty 23-ounce flywheel weight. Then, for his birthday, came the CNC-machined SFB cases and an FMF Q-pipe. The other extras made his ride more eyeworthy and his ride more comfort-worthy. He had two new headlights, head and tail, ready for the night-riding he had been promised, and he really wanted to do. He tucked his hands inside the bright yellow wraparound handguards which had saved him from constantly grazed, sore knuckles and stiff, mud-caked gloves. If he hadn't already known this pain he might have thought these particular accessories a bit soft. But aching hands slowed you down in the end. In a sport where, getting on and staying on and riding as far and as fast as possible was all that mattered, any extras were acceptable.

* * *

Charlie's Dad came in through the top farm gates kicking off wisps of straw that clung to his muddy boots. In his arms he carried a leggy, new-born lamb whose eyes seemed so much bigger than his head.

'Poor little mite,' said Mr Booking. 'Louise will have to look after this one, it's too cold and wet out here.'

Charlie peered at the lamb through his helmet visor and muttered, 'Perfect weather for me though littlun. I'll see you when I come back.'

'Where are you off to then, somewhere with the club?'

'Yes, Dad.'

'Good, you make sure you stick with them, then you'll be safe.'

'Safe, I hope not,' Charlie laughed his loud laugh and, as he did so, he threw his head back. There was a break in the clouds which revealed a buzzard soaring with its wings half extended ready for a stoop. It was in an Angel-Stoop position just like the angle of Charlie's elbows over his risers.

'Pee-yow, pee-yow,' came clear through the air. Then, like a ship in a heavy storm, it plummeted sideways and was gone. Charlie's Dad held the lamb a bit tighter feeling its fear. He hurried across the yard to the thatched farmhouse shouting back, 'See you later for tea, your cousin will be here about five.'

Charlie remembered the conversation he had had with cousin Luke last night on the phone. Luke said that he was

bringing his bike down from London on the train and, when he had asked Charlie how his bike was, he hadn't got an answer. Charlie had just turned the same question about his bike round to Luke. But petrol-hating Luke had persisted forcing Charlie to reply, 'It's a surprise, you'll see when you get here.'

'I'm looking forward to riding in the lanes again like we did last time.'

Luke gabbled on about the twisty green lanes so familiar to Charlie but so thrilling to Luke, the towny.

'Yes but…' Charlie tried to interrupt to tell him there and then that the bike he was talking about now was no longer a BMX.

'Yes but…' he tried again and got no further, even Charlie's booming tones were ignored as Luke prattled on about the green lanes which ran all around the farm. How was he going to put up with this for a week! He remembered how his cousin talked over him when he was speaking, even though everybody thought he was a nice quiet boy from the town. There was a silence and Charlie hadn't wanted to hold the information back. He had really wanted to tell him there and then that he'd now got a trial bike, with an engine, and that his mountain biking days were over. But that would have meant listening to more prattling.

'So what's it like?' Luke persisted.

'You'll just have to wait and see.'

He felt like the clever one now and not the stupid country cousin who didn't know anything. His town cousin seemed always to know more about the countryside than he did.

'All right, see you tomorrow, bye.'

Charlie had put the phone down with memories of this supposedly quiet relative coming into their country life for a while and leaving again in a hurry, with his Auntie Carol and his Mum, fussing over them and laughing. But that wouldn't happen this time.

He thought too about his visits to Luke's house in London when he had been younger and of how Luke had only wanted to talk about birds and flowers and country things while Charlie had wanted to go out into the streets so full of buses, lorries, cars and, of course, motorbikes. All different makes of motor bikes and outfits too.

He didn't have much in common with his cousin really. His Dad had sent for him saying,

'He can keep you company over half-term week when I'll be busy lambing.'

Charlie couldn't argue with this and knew that it was his Dad's way of doing everything he could for him now that Mum was no longer living with them.

'He'll be here about five,' said Mr Brooking.

'How long's he staying, Dad?'

'Nearly a week, going back on Saturday.'

Charlie had his helmet on now and just nodded. He

looked through his goggles up into his Dad's anxious eyes and shouted out, 'Yes, I'll keep all the gates shut, I know.'

There had been an increase in sheep and now lamb rustling going on in the farms in the valley, that's why his Dad was so worried. Charlie swung up onto the bike and, with a ramrod leg movement, pumped it into action. He liked to do it this way even if it didn't always work. It just felt right. He was off at no speed at all really, just enough to let his back wheel spin in the corner of the bend which led him out into the lane. Now here came the rain right in his face. He was on his way to an early morning hare and hounds meeting set up by the best rider in the club. This was perfect weather. It had been raining for days and Charlie knew that he was less likely to mire himself in the gloop now.

His technique of induced power slides was getting better every day. As he cruised along his shoulders brushed off bright yellow pollen from the overhanging hazel branches of the first green lane he turned into. There was a bit of a hard surface along here; a narrow line of cobbles either side, a morass of mud in the middle. He steered into this but was well aware of the problems. Half a mile ahead he would have to pull a wheelie to get out of this gloopy rut. When he first started riding, only six months ago on his sixteenth birthday, this was where he'd first tumbled. He'd rifled up into the air. Luckily his bike had cut out on impact with the solid ridge of cobbles.

He had gone forward, clean into a patch of brambles; the bikes behind him had piled up. The riders had to wait for 'Big Bog' to come along and remove his bike from the track. 'Big Bog', a giant of a rider, just slung his bike off the lane, as if it were a twig, roughly checked him out for injuries and threw the bike at him again with a surly, 'You're alright Charlie. Off you go.'

Even cheeky Charlie dare not speak out against 'Big Bog', so off he went wondering if he'd be banned from the club now.

It was his first outing and all had been going so well. He had felt embarrassed by holding up the team so near to the beginning.

He had learned a lot since then and now he knew how to change from one level of surface to another. Of course he always had known really. He had been doing it perfectly well on his MB since he was six. He was in an upright position, his knees slightly bent leaning towards the frame, head bent forward, eyes concentrated on the track, never raised any higher than half-way up the hedgerow.

He looked like a buzzard on his perching post leaning forward scanning for prey.

The sun came through the clouds as it does on spring days spreading warmth across his shoulders. Time for a Charlie whoop of excitement. He was out on the tarmac road now, quite close to town and heading for another

green lane entrance about 300 metres to the right. He slowed down a little to take the curve into the lane and then he had a go at getting his knee down, gliding round the bend like the dirt track racing bikes he had seen at Exeter – the Falcons. He shouted out, 'The Falcons, the buzzards the hawks – watch out all you beauties, Charlie's going to send you flying!'

2 COUSINS AT CROSSWAYS

Luke wondered why his mother had been so insistent about his bike being cleaned before he put it on the train down to Devon. Still, he had done as she wished, and now here he was plastering it in red mud on his way to Uncle Dan's. After his mother had dropped him off fussily at the station, he had phoned his Uncle, 'It's alright Uncle Dan. I can make my own way to Crossways. I know the way.'

Luke took the green lane which he remembered led to Crossways. There was nothing cross about the farm he thought; but with Auntie Sue gone maybe that was no longer true.

Once in the lane he wasn't so sure that it was the right one. The trouble was they did all look the same at first. He shot down the green tunnel, grateful for his crud race pack chain guard and crusher front and rear mudguards which were deflecting the red Devon dirt-spray and chicken-shot. He took the first berm gracefully, perfectly

balanced and said to himself, 'Thanks Dad for building my bike up to be this keen machine.'

It was a wonder he had got it finished at all with the constant interruptions from his Mum crashing through the hall to take Marmite the dog for a walk. Then Marmite walking off with his cable leads instead of his own. Then there was his sister pushing all his disc break layout, ready for assembly, under the hall stand just so that she could get to her shoes. Screws went missing for days. As for Sprocket the cat bopping the pedals round in the middle of the night and waking everybody up – well, tempers were frayed. He had the feeling that his family were glad to see the back of him and his bike for a week so that they could have the hall to themselves again for a while.

However, they had done it and here was this super light machine. The seat post was just 21 inches high, a bit awkward when you weren't sitting on it. He wasn't going in for any hard tailing so had fitted up the sus. to get the sag just right using an IRD (Intelligent Ride Dynamics) system. The riser was perfect and the leaf green paint was cool. When he took to the air on a drop off, from the green lane to the minor road, he felt like a buzzard soaring with wing tips curved slightly upwards. He lowered them for his stoop to follow through with a freeride. Perfection!

The route now took him through woodlands. He remembered it now. It was along here somewhere. There was a gap in the hedge. This was where they had built

jumps, rock gardens, rooties, step ups, and invented a few great drops. They had given them names like Stumpdance, Heart of Darkness and Roots of Evil.

Now the roots of the trees really kept him on the bounce. This was the bit that Luke hadn't been keen on at first because, where he lived, in West London, there were a lot of lime trees growing up out of the pavements. Their roots look like superman's fist smashing through glass, waiting to grab you and bring you down. He couldn't turn his bars tight enough. But now, with his reformed bike, these in Devon seemed easier to weave around – hurrah!

'HURRAH!' He shouted out as loudly as Charlie would.

This was real MB country and he was here for a week.

Something caught his eye behind the hedgerow as he pulled up at the lane bottom where a stream crossed the track. It was the downward rolling flight of a buzzard which looked set for a crash landing but coolly climbed up again to the tree tops of the wood which covered the hill to the side of the lane. As he hovered another buzzard swept up from the far side of the wood and roller-coasted down its boundary. They called to each other with their plaintive pee-ows from either side of the wood.

Oh yes, this is what he remembered about buzzards here – their complete dominance and mastery of their place. No cars here to push them into the corner of a field and out over motorway verges to compete with kestrels. No, here they were top dogs. Top birds.

He picked up his bike and silently made his way through the trees to the edge of the wood. The buzzards had roller-coasted off now, but he felt sure they would be back to what they had marked out as their territory, just over half a mile.

As Luke stood slumped over his handlebars taking in the stillness and peace of this scene there came the sound of a chain saw in the distance. Not so bad, he thought, at least it's a country sound, someone working in the woods and not digging up the road with a pneumatic drill.

He turned his bike round and headed back up a bit. Was it here where they had made their first rootie, he

thought.

Then out loud, 'I can't remember the route of the rootie!'

He stood up on his pedals. They were clipless platform downhill freeride ones with a magnesium platform, sealed cartridge bearing and cro-mo axles. They weighed just 580 grams and had replaceable pins.

He told himself to keep it light – let the wheels bounce just like Grant Ferguson, who had ridden for the Olympic games in Rio.

Wasn't there just one more big drop off here to bring him back flying into the lane?

He powered up the sloping hedgebank and took off. In mid-air the roar of the saw got louder. This was some giant chain saw and it was on wheels! It knocked him sideways, flashed across in front of him then crashed. Luke had stalled his landing and grounded. He was standing up on his pedals, the cleats holding him fast as he peered into the brambles at the sprawled shape of a trail bike. There was no movement. The sun cut through into the glade where the rider lay with his eyes closed, his goggles magnifying the weak spring sunshine, spreading the warmth all over his face.

That change of camber had brought him down again. This was something that never happened when he was on his MB – just a question of practice really. He shook his body – nothing broken. Dad needn't know. The next

thing that happened had nothing to do with fear of his Dad, just annoyance.

Who was this boy staring down on him from out of nowhere and trying feebly to lever his bike away from his body. Oh no – it was him, here already.

'It's all right, Luke. I'm OK,' said Charlie scrambling to his feet.

'Hello Luke.'

His voice was muffled and only his eyes were visible under his helmet, goggles and scarf.

Luke, surprised at hearing his name from a traillie, stood back and asked:

'Who are you then?' Why should a trail biker in Devon recognize him? He had seen one or two in the lanes last time he was here and some had dropped in at the farm for tea. But why had they remembered me, he wondered.

'Luke, it's me, Charlie.'

His voice rang out as his head escaped from the swaddling gear.

'Charlie? Oh, it's you. Hello. Are you OK? I didn't know you were riding…'

There was a pause while Luke struggled for words and settled sneeringly with, 'one of these.'

'Well, trying to, as you see. But what are you doing here? I thought you were coming later.'

'I caught an earlier train. So, this is your surprise. This is it.'

'Yeah, it's great don't you think?'

Luke's first thought really was that he didn't like the orange and red colours; his bike was leaf green to blend in with the countryside. Charlie stood back to admire his steed. He pushed down the stand and propped it up against the side of the lane. This was the first time he had had to describe his bike to someone. Still, Luke probably won't know anything about motorbikes anyway. He might be a townee but what did he know about trials, enduros and dirt bikes, he could say anything he liked. Luke probably thinks scrambling is something to do with eggs, he's so keen on birds, and they come out of them, so here goes, 'It's got CNC machined SFB cases and an FMF Q-pipe. Great isn't it?' Charlie cheeped. He pointed towards the engine and the exhaust. Luke didn't know exactly where to look and just said, 'Yeah, great,' and nodded his head in agreement, and added, 'The tyres are really nobbly aren't they?'

'Yeah, they are and then there's this flywheel weight see.' He pointed in the direction of the spokes, 'It looks heavy.'

'Heavy! This is one of the lightest bikes on the road,' he added doubtfully.

'I think so anyway. It doesn't matter with motors, it's not like MBs. You never end up carrying them. They always carry you.' He tried to scratch the mud from off his trousers.

Luke didn't know what to say, so asked him again, 'You're all right then? Your engine just stopped. I was just going to drop into the lane when you shot out in front of me. Nothing broken? I expect you can hurt yourself really badly on these things. Not just the old scaphoid joint snapped in your wrist.'

He paused, 'I can see why you didn't want to tell me about this bike on the phone.'

'Yeah, I wanted to keep it a surprise.'

'From trails to trials eh.'

'Yeah right,' Charlie grinned.

'Tell you what though, please don't say anything about this to Dad.'

'Why not? Does he just think you're out on your MB?'

'Well, of course not. He bought this bike for me but I'm not meant to go out on my own. I told him I was going out with the club, that they were waiting for me at the end of the drive. It wasn't true. But I need to practice on my own…,' he paused. The vision of the tailback he had caused last time he bailed was still with him, 'It's the only way I'll make it into the club for real.'

'No Charlie, I won't say anything.'

A buzzard appeared on high, beating a slow, big, wing-flapping descent as he swooped down. He swept over the lane letting out an alarm call, 'Pi-jaa – pi-jaa.'

Luke turned away from his cousin to follow its flight. Could it really be Nickwing still here after two years?

'Still doing the old bird watching then?'

Charlie asked and went on in his loud booming voice, sounding a bit bad-tempered. 'If you really had to live here all the time these buzzard calls would drive you mad. There's a lot of them about this year. The sheep get scared.'

'Well we don't get many buzzards up our way,' Luke said quietly still trying to follow the buzzard's flight path.

'That's how it is. Now that Mum's gone, we've put all that looking out for them behind us.'

'But the buzzard's cry isn't that bad, not like seagulls.'

'Take it from me I'd rather hear a seagull any day, and so would the sheep.'

Luke gave his cousin a puzzled look which sent him back to the safety of his scarf, goggles and helmet, surely all the talk of buzzards carrying off lambs wasn't true, but ravens, yes.

Charlie remembered how annoying his cousin could be, much worse than the buzzards, with his insistence on talking about birds as if he were a professor. The buzzard, the seagull, the yellow-bellied sapsucker, the lesser spotted perky parrot. He just wasn't interested, so he changed the subject quickly, he didn't want to fall out with him straight away. He pointed to his leaf-green bike, 'How's your bike then?'

Luke bounced his bike up and down on the shockies. He let Charlie feast his eyes.

'That shocky looks good, I bet you can pull some really

good wheelies on that.'

'On tarmac yes, but I'm not sure about on the real rough stuff like you've got here yet.'

He leant the bike in Charlie's direction so that he could get a better view. He could be technical too so he went on, 'Well yes, the shocks are lightweight air-sprung with custom tuneable spring rate. You can preload them via twin adjustable air chambers. It means you can dial in the sag and spring rate separately, linear or progressive as you require for any type of terrain or track. They've got adjustable compression and rebound damping too – there's nothing you can't programme in'.

He bounced the bike up and down again.

'Want to have a go?' Luke offered.

Charlie resisted, 'Yeah, well, when I've got time – I really want to get going with the club and this bike though.'

'I'll smoke you out on yours sometime.' Luke grinned at his cousin.

'Maybe,' said Charlie, still staring at the green-framed bike with reluctant admiration.

He turned back to his machine and set it roaring into action again. Although he had snapped down his visor Luke could still hear Charlie's voice above the engine shouting at him, the words muffled by his gag.

'Shee you bash shere.' (See you back there).

Remembering what his father had said his muffled shout added, 'Lode the ates and you.' (Close the gates

behind you).

With that he left Luke standing in the lane, the smell of diesel fumes and the crunch of chicken-shot jumping up at him as he roosted away.

Luke mounted on his bike and headed down back into the lane following the noise of the bike in front of him.

Close the gates! Luke couldn't remember there being many of them anyway. Now he could see the slate-grey roof and clay-brown chimneys of Crossways through the trees. He expected to hear the dogs, Sugar and Spice, barking any minute now. Silence!

Maybe they were out on the farm. Here was the gate to the drive firmly closed so he had to dismount. He stood and looked at the farmyard, suddenly worried about what he was going to say to Uncle Dan now that Auntie Sue wasn't there anymore. The front door was open. He went quietly in and noticed the sound of something tapping rhythmically overhead, far away, up in the roof. Rats playing musical chairs, he wondered.

This time his visit was going to be different.

3 SKY-DIVING

The following morning Luke was pleased to see Jack at the farmhouse. Jack was Charlie's best friend and even though he was eighteen months older than him, he seemed younger, and his voice wasn't so loud. Jack and Charlie had both had trial bikes bought for them by their farmer Dads about three months ago, and here was Jack eager to go out trialing with Charlie. On seeing Luke Jack asked Charlie, 'I wonder how our old mountain bike track is going?'

'Oh I expect the others keep it going,' Charlie quickly replied. He was eager to get out in the yard and talk trail biking with his friend.

'I checked it out a couple of weeks ago,' Jack said, 'it looks as if someone is still using it, something's going on,' said Jack.

He turned to Luke and said, 'I'm off with Charlie now but later let's give the MBs a razz and crack out a couple of loops.'

'You're on,' grinned Luke.

'What about you Charlie?'

'Maybe.' He replied and went out slamming the living-room door shut. A few seconds after it opened and Charlie shouted to his cousin, 'Remember don't forget to close the gates when you go out.'

The reason for this strict gate closing was given over tea with Uncle Dan, Cousin Louise and Charlie. At first he had thought it was to keep the dogs in. But there were no dogs now, they had gone with Auntie Sue. It was because there had been a lot of sheep rustling going on in the valleys and so security was important because thieves with lorries could come at any time, even in daylight, and load up unsuspecting sheep and lambs. The police did

their best but the problem was growing. Luke stood in the middle of the living room with its big sofas and huge TV screen and empty dog beds and thought about what he should do next. Well if he was biking this afternoon then he'd go birding now. Outside, coming towards him, closing the gate securely of course, was Louise.

'Hello,' she said cheerily to Luke as he approached clutching hold of his new binocular tripod, last year's Christmas present. It had been rather expensive and the optic which went with it had not been threaded properly and had fallen off on first use so he guarded it carefully now.

'That's new, isn't it,' she asked.

'Yes, I broke it and I've only just got it back so I want to go and test it out here, want to come?'

'Well, yeah I'd like to but…'

He plonked down his tripod and pointed it skywards as quickly as he could. There were buzzards high up over ahead.

'Sorry Lou, look, they're sky-dancing.'

'Sky-dancing, that sounds like something out of Star Wars or one of Charlie's freeriding moves in his DVD collection. That'll be a treat for you.' She smiled and waggled a finger at him.

He went on fiddling with the 'scope, then motioned for her to look down the turned up eyepiece.

'Just focus on one bird and you'll see how it works. That

one to the far right, see. Now he's just tipping up his wings to keep him steady, like a conductor taking up his stick thing to conduct. Then he makes a flattened out V-shape. Now he drops through the air on stiff outstretched wings. The buzzard in front of him is keeping perfectly still in the air. Now, he's making a half-fold wing shape in the wind and he is turning in the air. Now he's stiffening up his wings. Watch, wait, wait, wait and there he goes, sky-diving down.'

He pulled the 'scope away from her,

'No, don't bother with that, he's up, again just watch. It's starting all over again. He's started the dance all over again.'

'I can see the other buzzard now, he's getting closer.'

'Yes, he or she is doing the same.' She turned to concentrate on them, and followed their pattern of hovering, turning, then diving, mirrored by the other pair of buzzards in the sky.

She went back to look down the 'scope and said, 'This stands good, stops your arms aching.'

'It's easier to just look up once you've got them in your sight,' Luke said sympathetically.

'It's Nickwing. I saw him yesterday, look at him up there surviving with his old wing injury, that V-shaped nick in his wing span.'

'He's still got those markings underneath', Louise said. 'Those little brown rings on the outstretched wings. They look like eyes. They mesmerize the poor voles and shrews

down below.'

Luke stopped looking upwards and stared at his well-informed cousin as she went on, 'When they're in a stunned state of trance, they freeze, and that's that – well, that's what the experts say, but I don't think I've ever seen it actually happen.'

Luke looked up again, 'That's his mate, Smooth Soarer, and last year's fledgling.'

Louise disagreed. 'No, that fledgling will have its own territory now, and last year's mate would have moved on. This is a new mate muscling in on Nickwing's old territory – good luck to him.'

Looking upwards, Luke gurgled as he spoke, 'Let's call him Angel Stoop.'

With their heads bent upwards they started to walk back to the farmhouse.

* * *

In the afternoon Jack and Luke met up at the entrance to the farm.

Charlie turned up too with his old MB bike caked in mud; he'd never had a crud catcher. Luke's mouth dropped open at the sight of Jack's bike.

Jack's bike was one of those 29ers with bigger, chunkier wheels than most MBs.

'What d'you think?'

Jack pulled the riser up and down so that Luke could see the shockies in action.

'Big, big wheels,' shouted Charlie in his big, big voice.

Jack lent forward and pointed to the lettering round the rim, 'Bronson 29 by 22.'

'What's the ride like?' Charlie asked, throwing his old bike down in distain and stepping forward towards the 29er.

'Well,' said Jack, leaning possessively over the risers.

'I could even give the traillees a run for their money 'cause when this gets powering I can work this front end hard. This is a rough-smoothing, high-traction single-track steamroller.'

'Let's have a go, please.' Charlie begged.

'No, not yet,' Jack replied.

'You just watch how I handle it first. See this short stem and tapered head tube it gives a direct feel to the steering. Watch.'

Off he shot with his weight over the front end in a full on bulldog position. Luke thought how this always

reminded him of a buzzard's angel stoop.

'What a chunky beast,' he said. 'What a lot of hardtail fun.'

Charlie looked at his cousin puzzled that this bird geek seemed to know so much about bikes. He sheepishly picked up his old one. Here was a new world of MBs which he really liked. Had he swopped too soon?

'This bike hasn't seen much action in a while. Let's go.'

With his arms fully extended on the risers and his pedals hard down he roosted away. Luke swung round behind him, 'I'll follow you, I can't remember how it went.'

'It's a leg burner first up to Trant's Brake then we turn off at the top there along what used to be the fire road.'

Luke zig-zagged his weight up to ride alongside Jack so that he could hear what he had to say.

'The fire road. That was a bit of a problem. I don't think that old farmer liked us building kickers and whoops all over it. But he never had a fire in those woods so he never even knew we were there for ages.'

It was a fine day and as they reached the brow of the hill the watery February sun shone down over all the valleys, lined up like pop-ups on a screen. Jack stopped and pushed his bike through a gap by a gate at the top of the wood.

'You could get a fire engine through here anyway without going through the gate.'

The fire track was made up of broken stone and

crushed slate. They soon began to descend.

'This is going to be one downhiller,' Luke shouted excitedly.

They picked up speed and just as they were getting going a large fallen tree trunk growing vertically out of the hedge came into view. It had half blocked the way and was too high to bounce over and too low to skim under. Jack went to the hedge edge and wheeled his bike half way along the trunk until he was over the track again. Yes, it could be done so he went back up the trunk again and rode swiftly along it. When he was over the track he shouted out, 'Here comes the kicker.'

He balanced for a second on the tree's slippery surface, twisted the bars, and then, crashed down onto the path again. Luke was right behind him. Jack yelled out, as the path divided, 'To the left, go to the left.'

There didn't seem any way to go to the left, the track just ended. With remembered confidence Jack went flying in the air over a jump which spanned an eight foot gap of brambles and scrub below. Luke followed right behind.

They both drew up alongside each other now and stared ahead at a set of two feet to four feet high undulating muddy bumps of earth irregularly set out. They had hit the flick-flap whoops.

They threw themselves over them, wobbling and crashing into each other, laughing and shouting.

After this wide section they went into a single track

weaver through pines as straight as matches in a box. Luke tailgated Jack all the way.

Then there was a glade with a very muddy surface leading off at an angle which seemed to be blocked by piles of brushwood. It was a glade perfect for buzzards to soar over and then stoop down for their prey.

If Luke had held his own up until now he knew that he had been dealing with things he had met before. But not now the way the road just seemed to disappear ahead of him on a tight S-bend left him breathless. But he followed Jack's lead as he accelerated towards it and yes, the slide on the back wheel pulled him out of the berm and round again just in time.

He thought he heard some pigeons flapping out of the trees behind, but it was probably Charlie trying to keep up.

It wasn't over yet. Now the steepness of the hillside increased and they could make out the first of the obstacles to be woven round in this downhill slalom.

This time screens of hazel had been set at ten foot intervals down the track. Jack started to weave in and out, in and out, in and out, making sure his wheels never stopped spinning or he would have to bail. He was thankful that a screen was missing at the end of the drag or was this the beginning of the downhill free ride?

They had done it. Jack and Luke bounced all the way down to the bottom where they raised their handlebars

upwards in victory wheelies.

'It's still here, it's still nearly all here,' yelled Luke in disbelief.

He was thinking of how things got moved around at his circuit in his nearest patch of woodland back in London.

'I told you no one really bothered coming up here much now and, anyway, some conifers have gone, a whole block was felled last winter.' Jack said.

Luke gave him a blank look. Surely the MB gang didn't want their trail to be exposed by the disappearance of these trees.

'What do you mean?' he asked.

'It's the pine trees which are more likely to catch fire so

that's why they took them out.'

'Lucky for us.'

What they could not see, standing further back from the fire road, was one magnificent Monterey Pine tree, Nickwing's nesting lookout. Charlie hadn't been able to keep up with them from Franscombe Steep. Now here he was, creaking up beside them.

'I think I need to look at these shockies,' he said trying to bounce his bike. He looked exhausted and shocked when Jack said, 'Let's have another crack at it and see what's missing.'

'Is there an easier way up?' asked a tired Charlie.

'There is, we'll just take ourselves back down onto the road and loop up again. But it's a leg burner all the way.'

'Yeh, I can see that. Still downhilling is all about uphilling,' said Luke.

With this in mind they took a few moments to inspect their bikes for damage and shake their limbs about from the impact of the whoops and jumps. Now that the adrenaline had eased off Luke said, 'I thought there was a drop-off on this route, there was, because I bailed on it a few times. I remember.'

'A drop-off. Yes, you're right, that's what's missing and I can't remember where that was now.'

'Second time down will help us,' said Luke.

'Probably,' said a reluctant Charlie as they all swung up onto their pedals again ready to suffer.

They toiled away in silence up the side of the hill. There was no traffic about, no marching platoons of ramblers or road blocking horse riders to contend with.

Yet all the time they worked up and down the track a sharp pair of eyes had been watching them through the trees on the edge of the wood.

After they'd downed for what felt like the hundredth time and found the drop-off, just after the chicane, and which had been covered in nettles they sat down for a bit in the sun. Then, of course, the buzzards started their sky-dancing. It wasn't going to be easy for Luke to go ahead with the restoration of this MB trail. He knew that it would be a great thing to do and Jack was up for it, and maybe Charlie would join him on it before the holiday was over. But then there were the buzzards, who seemed to be nesting on the edge of this wood, but he couldn't be sure. Jack followed Luke's eyes upwards and guessed what he was thinking.

'So, what if there is a nest – it's not going to be on the ground, is it? Those old birds are used to us anyway.'

'Right, the nest will be at least 130 metres up, close to the trunk, probably in one of those conifers that the farmer has still left standing, maybe further into the wood.'

'It's not as if we're going to make a kicker that high now, are we?'

He laughed at Luke's worried expression and went on,

'Anyway how long do the chicks stay in the nest?'

'Fledglings, they're called fledglings and they won't fully leave until August.'

'The fledglings,' Jack struggled with the word and remembered what Charlie had said about his cousin being a bit of a professor type.

'They'll be in the nest all that time?'

'Well, they won't be in it night and day, of course, they'll be flying by then but they'll still come home to roost.'

'They'll be fine whatever we do down here. And we only ever come about once a week for a couple of hours, and we're not as noisy as scramblers that's for sure.'

'I suppose not, but it is a disturbance.'

'Yeah, I agree with you on that. Look how big they are, how cool, how at the top of their food chain they are. Nobody can harm them. Nobody ever shoots them now.'

Luke got onto his bike again as he didn't really want to go on spouting out all he knew about these birds. He didn't want Charlie's mate thinking he was a wimp or a swot, or a bit of a prof even.

'Come on, let's sort out that drop off, we'll get some sticks and thrash those nettles back into the ground.'

And with that Luke picked up his super lightweight bike and headed back into the woods, jumping over the ditch in one leap. Over through the trees in the clearing he saw a buzzard perching on the top of a tree stump. It turned its head almost right round at the sound of the boys' voices. He could see that it had a shrew or vole pinioned in its pale talons. Those craggy claws were almost the same colour as the under-plumage. In defiance it tipped its tail and glided away to tear its prey apart on the forest floor far away from human eyes.

4 'BUTEO BUTEO' AND THE BEAST

Charlie cut out his engine at the farm gate and pushed his bike over the yard to the stables. His sister, Louise was coming down the farmhouse path and reached the garden gate just as Luke rode into the yard. He stopped to chat.

'What are you going to draw out here?'

'I've been drawing, finished now. I was just coming out here to put some pictures in the car, my portfolio, for school tomorrow. Luke came over.

'Can I see?' he asked.

'If you want, they're nothing special.' She opened the purple folder and flicked through some views of the house and some fishermen with nets on a beach.

'Good stuff.' He smiled at her.

'Oh, not really, I just like sketching and some of it has to be done anyway for school.'

As she closed the folder the top picture stuck to the cardboard cover inside and its bold black outlines intrigued Luke.

'What's this?' he asked. She flicked it back quickly and then shut the folder tight. He had glimpsed a pen and ink sketch of a buzzard, in a 'half angel' position, wings inclined back, head forward in an aggressive pose. With the folder under her arm, she quickly changed the subject.

'I expect you're hungry, aren't you? Cream tea's coming up. All that exercise, makes you hungry.'

She looked over towards her brother in the stable block with his trial bike.

'Well, you anyway,' she nodded at Luke, 'you've been out cycling again, not just sitting on a noisy old machine for miles.'

Louise gave Luke a nervous smile and walked to the car. He wondered why she hadn't wanted him to see the buzzard sketch. It didn't look as if it had been copied from a book – it was too life-like. The thought of those gurt tubs of clotted cream tugged at his stomach and he started back towards the house. He went back into the stables to see if Charlie was coming too. Charlie had seen Louise showing her work to Luke and came over muttering through his helmet.

'Lou's good, I think, but she's quite secretive about her work'.

He added: 'She used to show Mum everything.'

He could only just make out what he said and didn't want to ask him to repeat anything about his Mum, his Auntie Sue. Luke's Mum had told him before leaving London not to say anything about Auntie Sue if he could help it. It seemed that she had had enough of farm life and had left just after Christmas. She wrote to them all, said she had gone on holiday but didn't say when she was coming back.

Charlie pulled his helmet off clumsily and looked inside it just to make sure his head wasn't still there and stared down at Luke's shining bike.

'I suppose it's difficult to hose down a bike in town, all those small stones and mud running into the neighbours' gutters. You can use this hose anytime you know.'

His trail boots clanked off over the cobbles to the side of the stables and he came back trailing a thin black rubber hosepipe with a silver-capped hose end, letting out sharp sprays of water as he approached the bike.

'Here, try this.'

Luke didn't want to refuse, even though he had just applied his special protective wet lube on his chain. Any sign of friendliness at the moment from his cousin was to be welcomed. His Mum had said that he would be upset and that it would be difficult. He gingerly took the nozzle and sprayed down the riser bar. Charlie snatched it out of his hand.

'No, not like that. Open it right up, give it some wellie.'

With a broad grin Charlie jumped back and turned the nozzle onto Luke's legs making him jump up and down like a chicken. So this was the game. Luke grabbed the bucket full of dirty water standing by his bike and chased Charlie to the other end of the stable where he launched the water in a great stream all over him. This was fun. He suddenly stopped feeling like a wet blanket and became one. He clattered towards the farmhouse door. The cleats on the bottoms of his mountain bike shoes held him back; especially designed to hold your feet in place and move with the ride, they weren't any good on a quick getaway run from an annoying cousin.

* * *

Life in the farmhouse did feel different now that Auntie Sue was gone. He dared not ask about the dogs called Sugar and Spice who once lived there. Still, everyone was very busy farming and Luke really liked that. This evening when his Uncle Dan disappeared back to the cows and the lambing shed, and Charlie went off to help him, he could go wandering off to the woods on his own. Or, if Louise was about, he could just spend time feeding the big open fire in the living-room with various pieces of gnarled seasoned timber, slices of newly felled ash and wedges of sweet chestnut that spat onto the hearth. They only had central heating at home. The room smelt of damp logs and the faint scent of daffodils, huge bunches of which stood in vases lit up in the dying embers of the

sun coming through the smeary window panes. Louise appeared and he asked about the sketch which she had hidden away earlier.

'I liked the buzzard outline.'

'Not mine, I copied it.'

'Copied it from what?'

'Something else,' she snapped back.

He didn't want Louise to start treating him as Charlie did and snapped back too.

'Copy, yes I do know what the word means.'

He stood up suddenly and said 'Come on, let's go and see what they're up to. It'll stay light for a while yet.'

'Who?'

'The buzzards again, of course, just over in the woods.'

'There aren't as many this year,' she said.

In what he thought to be a country accent he said, 'Has that old gamekeeper been at them with his gun?'

'What gamekeeper? There isn't one any more. It used to be Radley's Dad but he's dead.'

'I'm pleased to hear it. He used to think that buzzards were really responsible for killing young pheasants and partridges even though they never found any evidence. He just carried on trapping and shooting them,' Luke said. Realizing what he had said he added, 'Sorry, I mean I'm not really glad to hear that the gamekeeper has died. Poor Radley.'

They were out along the path behind the farmhouse,

having shut the gates securely behind them. Louise said, 'We've got to be careful, the sheep rustlers are about.'

Then she carried on talking about the buzzards. 'We used to find dead ones in the woods and the fields. Such big birds just lying there and being pecked about by rooks and ravens who could just shrug off most of the time when they were alive.'

He didn't like to look at her because he could hear tears and anger in her voice.

'I hope it's not happening again,' Louise said.

'Exactly what is happening again?' he asked.

'Well shooting, killing anything which the shoot managers think might harm their precious birds.'

Luke wondered just how much she knew and didn't want to upset her with tales of death. He had read that some buzzards were lured down to rabbits which had been injected with strychnine. It killed foxes, weasels and stoats too.

'You haven't found any dead birds recently have you?'

'No, but you can't be sure what's going on out here. It's difficult to know who to trust.'

'What about your Dad, he knows everybody involved in the shoot doesn't he, he knows who's looking after the birds?'

'Just which birds are we talking about here, the pheasants or the buzzards?'

'Oh, the buzzards, for sure.'

She grabbed at some grass and started to shred it in her hands as she spoke.

'The buzzards. He knows they don't do any damage. Even if he never saw what Mum was doing, never read anything she wrote. We know he really knew.'

She paused and threw the grass on the ground.

'There were rows.'

Once more there were tears in her voice and, although he wanted to know more about what his Auntie Sue had been doing, he just handed her his binoculars, and looked upwards.

Pi-jaa – pi-jaa.

Ka'ka'ka'ka'.

'There they go soaring and counter-soaring in linking spirals following each other up. I've watched them for over an hour getting wider and wider apart.'

He pointed at an old stag-head oak with some brown foliage still clinging from its skinny top branches.

'I bet they'll end up there.'

As he said this there was a rustling in the hedgerow. They both looked round to see Radley emerging from the undergrowth and pulling off barb-like brambles as he came towards them. He was a scraggy-looking kid, about nine, dressed in a hoodie, old jeans and muddy trainers. A lick of red hair fell into his freckled face.

'Watch,' he said, and smiled his tooth-missing grin.

He looked up and blurted out in an embarassed way,

'I've seen as many as forty up there, but today's not a great day for it.'

'Rad.' Louise said, 'What are you doing here?'

'Well,' he paused, always a one to please others and to get on everybody's side he said, 'I was doing some mouse watching. Trying to save them before those buzzards swoop.'

'Stoop.' Luke corrected.

Louise then said, grinning at Luke, 'You can't do that, that's their dinner. Anyway they're not hunting now. They're sky-dancing.'

'Oh yeah,' said Luke with assumed knowledge again.

'Of course they are, sorry.'

'Where's Charlie?' he asked, feeling a bit nervous in front of Luke who he had met before but didn't really know very well.

'Don't know. In the lambing sheds maybe, don't know,' said Louise.

'I wanted to see him with some information, very interesting information.'

'D'you want me to tell him?'

'No,' he smiled mysteriously at Luke.

'It'll wait, just like the glow worm larvae in the mud, if no one disturbs them.'

'What are you on about now?' Louise asked because although normally she would just not take any notice of this little boy's ramblings, she didn't want to appear

rude in front of Luke who, apart from being her cousin, was a guest after all. Mum had always told them to be polite to guests. Radley was no guest, but he might have something interesting to say to Luke who was fascinated by anything to do with wildlife. Poor old Radley trying to get away from the hard line 'shoot every vermin' style game keeping his Dad had been so keen on. He knew a lot about trapping and poisoning but wished he didn't. He scooped up a handful of muddy earth from behind the hedge.

'There might just be some in here, this is what they like – a place that is behind something you see. Just like where those mountain bikes make berms on the bends, behind those there could be some glow-worm larvae waiting. They wait for up to three years before they come out. That is if they're not disturbed.'

In a kind of sneaky way he went over to Luke and said, 'If they're not disturbed by something more powerful, bigger, noisier.'

He darted an accusatory look at Louise too.

'What are you talking about? Tractors? We've got to go down the lanes to get to the fields. Hastercombe Estate uses them too.'

'S'ppose so,' he whined and threw the earth down.

'Ever seen glowies?' He questioned Luke.

'No.'

'Pale green little strips. You can collect them, put 'em in

a match box and use it like a torch.'

Luke became interested, 'Really!'

'Yeh, in the summer though, I can show you them in the summer.'

The buzzards let out their slightly aggressive tone above, long and slow. It was as if this were a cue for his disappearance so Radley dived back into the hedge and was gone.

'He's a strange boy that one, likes his wildlife, but doesn't seem to have any real friends,' Louise said.

She looked up again at the sky-dancers.

'Wish we could join them, don't you?'

'Yeah, but we can't, I sometimes think I know how they feel when I'm on a downhill, not an up-air spiral, on my bike. It's sort of like flying.'

'If you say so, but that seems as far away from what they're doing as...as....Radley's glow-worm larvae hiding away behind the berms.'

'What do you think we should call them?'

'Wrigglers, firebums, I don't know.'

'No, not glow worms, these buzzards?'

There were quite a few birds now circling in the sky above them.

'Well, that one has got to be Sky-Dancer, what a gyrator.'

'Then there's Wing-Clipper next to him.'

They were almost falling over backwards craning up into the sky.

'Then that one,' she pointed but Luke wasn't looking.

'Could be Sky-Soarer.'

'Followed by Angel-Stoop.'

He said, throwing himself down into the grass.

'Time for a bit of stooping down into that fridge. Race you back.'

As they ran back into the house Luke noticed, once more, the empty kennels just outside the back door. That dog emptiness which had first hit him when he arrived was all he really had to complain about so far.

Life at Crossways was still good.

5 DIRT JUMPERS AND ROOTIES

Charlie had returned from his farming duties now and was watching a traillee showing on the big TV in the living-room. He sat upright and alert on the sofa his eyes glued to the screen. It looked as if he could feel the revving on the start line vibrating up his legs and up through his stomach. He edged forward on the sofa as the riders let the throttles go, and ratcheted through the gears to get out on the straight. They rode, standing up on their pegs, their weight poised over the middle of the bikes, easing slightly to the rear. The wind hit them as they switch-backed onto the bend. Perfect.

Charlie now watched the leader, number 22, who was in the lead. He had just made it round but the blast cone of number 40's exhaust at his side jittering him inches ahead. The table-top was now in view. It gleamed covered in mud and oil. He burned into the up slope, swooping it up, flying for a split second of airtime, moving his body forward towards the front wheel. He landed on the front wheel, contact, steady, burn away. Just number 40 still out

there ahead of him. Number 22 going into third and on the pipe with his front wheel six inches off the ground. Overtaking, pelting tiny roost everywhere. Had he made a mistake by slamming on the binders as the drop-off approached? How high was he going to jump?

Now his weight was on the back wheel. Holding the throttle open he pushed gravity backwards for a rear wheel landing. In airtime he could see the racing line ahead, only some whoops and kickers to go and he had ridden them before, he recognized them from other parts of the track. He felt secure. He roosted away. Now he heard the crowd. Up went the chequered flag. He pulled a victory wheelie. He was the winner.

Charlie jumped up from the sofa. 'Look at that, the clear winner.'

'It was over so quickly,' said Luke.

'It's a short loop, you loon, that's why.'

He shouted up at him and laughed. 'D'you see how he put the binders on?' Charlie asked.

Sitting on the arm of the settee he demonstrated.

'You put your weight over the rear wheel to get the grip then go down a gear, maybe two. You brake with the front brake lever and the rear brake pedal at the same time. But when you're starting a circuit you've got to be in the right gear for a quick getaway. Don't worry about those around you just drive straight on with your elbows out, don't let the others push you to the side. Work out where in a corner you're heading. Work out the ride in your head before you go but be prepared to change.'

He jumped down from thr settee and looking serious said, 'I know I have to do this because those club riders are so experienced, they hardly ever bale.' He brightened up.

'Well I know you townies are always looking for the peace and quiet of the countryside, so let's break it one more time,' said Charlie, starting the race again and turning up the roaring sound of the bikes.

'Who was the winner there, then?'

'Who? Who is he? Just the South West Champion, that's all. Did you like it? Could you stand to watch some

more? It's not so different from MBing really.'

* * *

Back on the MB trail the next day the gang had found somewhere to sit in the glade and started looking for their snacks. Luke drew apart from them a little to be followed by a pebble whizzing past his ear.

'Oh, I'm sorry, it wasn't for you, it was for that squirrel.'

'The squirrels. What's wrong with them?'

'What's right about the beasts. They strip the bark off the trees for a start. My Dad used to hate them,' said Radley.

One of Radley's Dad's chief responsibilities had been for Uncle Dan's woodlands.

Radley went on, 'Buzzards don't like them much either. They eat them you know,' he added with a ghoulish grin.

'Do we only eat things we don't like?'

As if in agreement to this strange question three buzzards who had just catapulted themselves into the air from the edge of the woodland, pee-yowed as much as to say well, actually we'll eat anything that comes our way, like it or not.

'How can we ever know if animals are friends with what they eat?' asked Eustacia, commonly known as Useless, which was bad luck on a girl who really knew how to slam it on when going downhill.

'Last spring I saw the mangled remains of a squirrel hanging from a buzzard"s nest in the New Forest when

we was on holiday. Didn't look like they were the best of friends.'

While the others got on with eating Luke took out his binoculars to check out the group of birds soaring higher and higher. Eustacia worked her way to his side.

'What else do buzzards eat then?'

'They'll have a go at anything really, little birds like chiff-chaffs, woodpigeons and doves. Wood mice, robins, frogs, lizards, moles and even insects like beetles.'

'Are you telling me they can see beetles crawling in the grass from right up there.'

'No, they don't hunt them like that. They use the same techniques as other birds, running and stamping along the earth to imitate rain. Because they do eat anything they always survive.'

Radley, eavesdropping on the conversation, shouted across. 'There are some things they eat which won't help them to survive.'

Luke gave him a puzzled look, but was distracted from asking more by Eustacia almost snatching his bins from him and then asking, 'Can I have a look?'

'Help yourself,' he commented and went over to the other bikers. He shouted back at her Charlie-style, 'Those buzzards are in their zone now hunting from mid-morning to late afternoon. They'll wander away in the morning and evening. That's when you'll see scraps as they stray into other birds' territories.'

With the sounds and sights of the trial still echoing in his head from the night before he just had to ask, 'So, how fast do you really think MBs can go downhill on the rough?'

A straggly-haired mate of Jack's replied, 'Oh, I reckon at least 35.'

'Have you got a speedo?'

Radley went over to Jack and said, 'Has he got a speedo – look at this. He's got one of those that link up to a computer, his Uncle bought it for him.'

Jack meekly handed over his wrist to Radley who pulled him over to show Luke. Jack did really have all the right gear and was just as good a rider on his MB as he was on his MX, but he was no show-off. He said nothing about the watch, but just offered some more information on Charlie's uncle.

'Charlie's got an Uncle. I think his name was Fred. He was very big on time trials on a bike and 24 hour races. Even when he was old he was doing over 350 miles in twenty-four hours non-stop.'

Everybody was looking sort of impressed and a bit blank at this but swarmed round when Radley, still holding Jack's wrist, started to explain how it worked.

'Look, it gives you speed, of course, but then splits it up into max speed and the average. Tells you the trip distance, the upper and lower limits of your heart rate and of course it's got GPS and maps if you want. It's got

five exercise profiles too.'

A body-armoured boy asked, 'So, have you ever downed Fratscombe steep in less than sixty seconds?'

Jack shook his wrist free from Radley, clenched and unclenched his brakes.

'Might have. Don't know.'

'Aren't you getting your MX speeds confused with your MB ones?' The warrior boy sneered.

'No, I'm not dazed or confused I know the difference. In fact riding an MX as well makes MB racing even more exciting. The speeds seem faster on these muscle driven ones.'

They all stood round now just waiting for Jack to take up the challenge, just waiting for him to show how fast he could go. He swung up onto his bike. 'I'll do it now if you like. I'll go first, the rest of you can follow.'

'Wouldn't it be best if we went first and checked it out and you timed us, then we could watch you come blazing through last, maybe?' said Luke.

'All right then, get going, I'll shout out get set, go, for each of you.'

With that there was a scramble to get their helmets, gloves and goggles on and they whooped off in a downhill direction.

At the bottom of the run a lake of water had gathered over the past week. The riders focused on the hump leading out of it and over onto the other side and leant

back as they hit the water. No one bailed. They loved the idea of being timed as the ice-cold sheets of spray surrounded them. How much this set them back they didn't know but there was Jack hollering away, his speedo would tell them the facts.

* * *

Louise slammed the phone down as Luke entered the room. She looked flustered.

'Oh, you've just missed your Mum – she sends her love.'

So why hadn't Louise let him talk to her?

'Oh, OK, I'll text her later.' He looked puzzled.

'It's strange she should call here, I mean, perhaps she

wanted to talk to your Dad? She always calls me on my mobile.'

'I don't know about that,' she went on, sounding as if she was trying to work something out.

'If one of my friends falls out with another one of my friends I won't stop talking to both of them.'

'D'you think that birds fall out with each other in the same way?'

'Directly, yes, over food or a mate, then and there, of course they do. What do you think it means when a buzzard's cry changes from pee..iowing to pee..ya? And why do they keep their wings stretched out a bit when they stoop?'

Louise suggested, 'No idea about the cries, but the wings they keep them free for control, to change direction'

Luke looked impressed.

'Yeah, you've got it. They fold their wings a bit and just go for it towards prey or an attacker.'

'So they fight for food and mates and territory. I just wondered if birds would fight for anything else. Still it's about the same for humans isn't it?'

Before Luke had time to reply she had flopped down onto the settee and, pushing all the magazines and DVDs aside asked, 'So, does my Mum come round to yours a lot. I liked, I mean like your Mum, Auntie Carol. We always had a good time when she came here. It was fun going out with the two sisters down to the river. They ran wild, and

so did we, said Louise.

'I remember.' Luke ventured.

'Is your Dad OK? Charlie obviously doesn't want to talk about what's happened.'

Louise said, 'He doesn't talk about anything really. He's gone very quiet, well, I know he's loud but… has he been talking to you then?'

'He talks bikes mainly and only when we're out. He seems to spend a lot of time on the bike stuff.'

He prized a traillee case, whose sharp edge had been sticking into him from the back of the cushion, and turned it over.

Louise suddenly said, 'Buzzards mate for life you know.'

'But their lives might only last for seven years on average, although longer livers have been found,' Luke said.

Louise logged into YouTube on the big screen in the living-room and read aloud, in a shaky voice, the gothic lettering. 'Nine lives, shall we try it. I'd never ask Charlie to watch it with me, he takes it all so seriously.'

'It's his, he won't mind?'

'Oh come on, he's gone out to a club meeting, he won't even know.'

They switched on the machine.

'Come on then – let's burn.'

They turned the sound off so that they could carry on talking to each other.

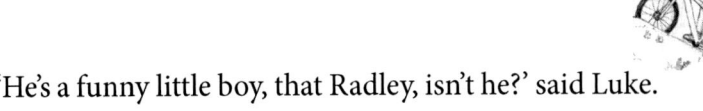

'He's a funny little boy, that Radley, isn't he?' said Luke.

'I suppose so. He's always hanging around, he's always out of it. A bit odd. He sticks up for wildlife now and then, well....' she paused.

'But then I find him doing things like making snares for rabbits. I caught him once in the woods over a smokey fire. He was holding the wire of the snare over the smoke so that it dulled over and didn't catch the light so that the rabbits wouldn't see it.'

Luke added grumpily, 'Or any other animal which might see and run straight into his death traps.'

Louise nodded in agreement, 'But I think he's OK. I like him really.'

Charlie and Uncle Dan came in just as the series of trials was ending. Charlie was excited and shouting something about a night ride coming up. His Dad looked grim.

6 'FOURPENCE FOR A BUSARDE'. HENRY VIII'S BLOOD MONEY

Luke was out riding on his own this morning. Charlie hadn't got up yet and he could hear Louise banging about in the attic again. He wondered why she was always up there.

So off he went for a ride around the village. There was a leg-burning hill up to the church from where another group of green lanes began. As he flip-flopped steadily up he saw an old lady, bent over a walking stick, making her way up to the church door. He stopped at the lych gate for a rest.

She saw him and shouted out, 'Young man, young man, come here, please.'

She sounded so much like one of his teachers in London that he propped up his MB and went meekly towards her. He was greeted by the excited twitter of

sparrows and blue tits in the trees where half a dozen bird feeders were hanging.

She waved her stick towards the yew tree.

'You see, I just can't quite reach up into those three there. I'll get the nuts and you can help me please.'

'Ok, I can do that, I think.'

She went into a side door in the bell tower and Luke followed. There, on an old wooden table, was a large leather-bound book. It lay open showing columns covered in spidery black ink writing. She dived under the table and brought out a plastic tub full of peanuts. She poured some out into a wire bird feeder and took it over to the door. Luke was craning his neck over the writing.

'This looks really old,' he said, and peered down into the book. She told him that it was, and that in Tudor times, five hundred years ago when it had been written, because the population was rising, fields were smaller and more sheep were grazing. Fewer fields were used for growing grain for making bread. So corn and barley fields were precious and had to be protected against vermin and birds. Henry VIII had set up a law to reward those who helped to exterminate them. Elizabeth I had agreed with her Dad, Henry, so she passed the 1566 Act for the Preservation of Grain. The old lady glided up beside him, 'These are the Churchwarden's accounts.'

She lowered her voice and carefully turned over the pages, 'Poor little things.'

She looked up, listening to the birds outside and Luke wanted to get back out there quickly, but she bent her head over the tome again and followed the text with her bony finger.

'Don't worry, I can reach the feeders I'll…do it right away,' Luke suggested but she ignored him.

'Just look what used to go on: *To Henry Trant, sixpence for the heads of thirty crowes, at a penny for five. Thruppence for 36 stares heades at a penny for twelve.*'

'*Stares?*' Luke questioned.

'Starlings,' she went on, 'fourpence for a busarde.'

He interrupted excitedly, 'Is that a buzzard?'

'Yes, *a busarde's head at four pence each, and two and a ha'penny for five egges each or, one penney for two.* Sometimes they'm written down as puttocks. Puttocks, the old Devon word for *Buteo buteo*.'

'What's this all about. Who was paying out this money for birds' heads?' he questioned indignantly.

'The landowners had to provide money to pay for those who came to them claiming to have destroyed "noyfull Fowles and Vermyn." But they'd only get their money if they produced the heads of their victims.'

'Buzzard's eggs are so lovely, he said, sort of oval, white not shiny, with red and brown-grey markings.'

The old woman flew at him, 'How d'you know that young man, how d'you know?'

'I've seen them, in books, once in a nest… '

She raised her arm: '…but I never touched them. No, don't think that.'

She stood angrily shaking her peanut bottle at him and stared. He felt nervous under her bird-like gaze.

'Here you are.' She passed him the feeder, 'If you're really interested we'll come back when you've hung this up and I'll tell you more. But remember people had to survive, they had to make a living where they could then. They needed all that grain to make bread.'

Now she really sounded like his London history teacher.

'They didn't know if it was right or wrong to destroy God's creatures. She stabbed at the page. 'Look, not just birds *but heads of Grays, badgers for 12d and for 12*

rattes or myse heads 1d. But here's one I don't mind. *One halfpenny for the heade of everie Moldewarpe or Wante.*'

'Moldewarpe or Wante?' Luke questioned.

'Yes, moles what do dig up our lawns and any grassland' She cackled, 'and sometimes these graves.'

She flitted out of the church with Luke following. He filled up most of the feeders but was finding it difficult to reach the topmost ones. He wondered how this little woman by his side could manage without the help of passing strangers. He thought of Freestyle tricks he had seen on Charlie's TV and, passing the bottle back to the old lady, said, 'Hang on to this. I'll get my bike.'

He balanced on the bars while the old lady hung onto the frame tightly. He cycled his way from tree to tree and with a shout jumped down on top of a grave mound. He quickly stepped aside.

'Thank you, young man. What's your name? I'm Miss Trant, pleased to meet you.'

'I'm Luke, Charlie Brooking's cousin, I'm staying with my Uncle Dan at...'

'Oh indeed,' she said, a little frostily before he had finished, 'then you'll know all about bird destruction anyway.'

Before he could ask her what she meant exactly, she had gone, closing the little door in the tower behind her.

* * *

Back on the green lanes again Luke was looping over

the other side of another wild area of woodland cut through by tracks. He hadn't met a walker, a horse-rider, certainly no MXs or MBs or seen a house, a barn or a hut for miles it seemed. He felt that he had lost the track but he kept going all the same. He crossed over a green lane and into a patch of scrub. He pushed through and found himself looking down into a chasm of a lane. Could he get to the bottom and find out where it went? He'd give it a go. Good job he had mitts on, not as clumsy as Luke's fancy handlebar cuffs but more thorn-proof. These were the business Altura Pro Gel Mitts with a strategically positioned 'gelcell' pad to protect the ulnar nerve. He pulled his bike half-way down, left it there and jumped down into the well of the green lane. Then he pulled the bike down on top of him, his helmet took the weight of the hub. He straightened himself up as he sprung the bike round upright and bounced on its shocks. It was very dark and quiet in the lane.

So where to now? Any direction would do to get him out more easily than he had come in.

He clattered and swerved along for a while. The rock garden surface made the going tough despite his knobbler tyres. There was a break in the bank to the left and a set of newly constructed steps led up the bank side. He stopped, propped up the bike, and climbed up into the light again.

There looming, or rather leaning, at the side of the lane, he saw the outline of a black wooden garden shed.

He hesitated. Outside the door was a flat area concreted over. Luke pulled off his helmet and picked out a squashed packet of cigarettes from his anorak. This was something no one knew about him, and he didn't know why he was still doing it. When this packet was empty – that would be it, he told himself. This looked like a good place for a quiet smoke with none of his family as witnesses.

Sunlight fell on the door so he sat down on the concrete platform in front of the hut with his back against the door inhaling the smoke and the sun's rays. He bent his head back towards the warmth and as he did so he found himself eyeballing the wizened talon of a bird. He jumped up and there were more remains of dead creatures all nailed to the door like some weirdo's cloakroom closet. Because of their blackened, shrunken state it was difficult to identify any of the creatures clearly. He recognized ferret, squirrel or stoat pelts, foxes and badger paws, rook and raven heads, kestrel and maybe buzzard talons dangling on this gibbet door. He stumped out his cigarette and moved away from the hut. A large rain cloud moved over the sun and, as he swung back up onto his MB, the sound of tapping came muffled through the black door. He was off.

It was time for him to go and meet up with the others again. Sometimes the silence, or the odd sounds of the country, got to him when he was alone. He rode down to the meeting point.

Luke bent down to get a drink from his flask, but it

wasn't there. He was surprised as it was one of the extras he had made sure would never fall off. He had worked out a contraption to fix it firmly in place wherever he was, on whatever hairy circuit he might travel over. But it wasn't there. Could he have lost it in that sunken lane or by that black hut?

* * *

'What if we set up a circuit along the same loop as the MXs?' said Jack. Luke gave him a puzzled look.

'Why would you want to get tangled up with them?'

'I am anyway, just starting with a new Moto-Cross bike.'

'But I love my 29er best at the moment as you see,' Jack said. 'I think all these vehicles going up and down the lanes at the same time is really all about who has got the right to roam,' Luke said.

Jack paused to think. 'Everyone right? But nobody should be roaming in a way which stops others doing their roaming. And all this confrontation's got to stop.'

'Sounds like you believe in a little a-roaming-a-therapy Jack,'

'Luke, don't. It's serious.'

Luke was equally as serious about what was happening on the ground as about what was happening in the air. He cast his eyes upwards and there they were. Sky-Stooper and Angel-Stoop, just hanging in the air. Jack poked him.

'Hey you. I'm trying to have a serious conversation

here. I want to know what you think about this.'

Luke said, 'You know these buzzards soaring about in the sky. They are not always doing it for any particular purpose. They're doing it just because they can. Maybe they are doing it for fun.'

He looked down, 'And you know that do you because that's what we're doing it for too. Just for fun.'

He held up his hand to stop Jack interrupting.

'I know. I know what you're saying, that if we destroy the atmosphere with CO_2 emissions as traillees do we should stop them. But maybe they should just use them less. We'll have to make our MB case stronger to show them that it's just as much fun. And if they want spills just watch how Grant Ferguson our MB champion bails and tumbles and yet gets up again. So, we've got to stand up for as much CO_2 free fun as we can. But I'm not sure that we should fight about it. After all petrol will run out one day.'

'I wish you were right,' said Jack, 'because I can't choose either. But it would be fun to block them on our own terms for once, don't you think?'

He did not reply immediately but looking up once again said, 'I met this old woman by the church and she had these records that showed how buzzards were hunted because they thought they were eating all the people's grain. See how wrong that was. Everyone knows it's small vermin like mice and rats that do that. But buzzards, so

they could have helped save the grain. We know that now, but then!'

He looked up again.

'Look at them, masters of their domain, they've won, but they don't need to keep telling us that they have.' He looked down again and then went back to Jack's idea of showing motor heads that MBs were as much fun.

'Block them, set up a drop off that only MBs could do, that would be too heavy for traillees, for example.'

Jack continued to shovel earth back up against the high bank of the drop-off.

'We could use the loops at different times, maybe watch each other. But who would sort that out? Not those at Hastercombe who manage the shoot. They're too busy making money and shooting their birds,' Jack said.

'I don't know,' Luke replied.

Pi-jaa pi-jaa pi-jaa-pi-jaa

'Ask them, they've always got plenty to say for themselves and they'll certainly have a bird's eye view over whatever happens next.'

* * *

Charlie's Dad was out in the woods too. He was always thrilled to see buzzards perching on trees and poles just out of reach of humans at an altitude which was laughably low for them. But how frightening would it be if you were down even lower than a human being and you were spotted in the undergrowth by a buzzard's sharp eyes,

there would be nothing beautiful about them then.

The 'Buteo, buteo' or as old Mrs Trant would say, 'the old beauties' were the best birds to see in these woods and valleys. They owned the territory, although humans and other creatures thought otherwise. Picking on buzzards was a common mistake made by inferior birds such as crows, rooks and jackdaws. He didn't want to be part of this persecution any longer. As he stopped staring skywards and started out for Crossways he saw a green and white drinking bottle lying in the lane, picked it up, wondered how it had got there then took a refreshing drink.

7 THE HUT IN THE WOODS

Back in the house Luke was on his own again, in the living room. If only Sugar and Spice were still here. Dogs are always up for fun, a bit of an outing, a play fight, whatever. But the dogs were definitely not here and there had been no attempt to replace them as far as he could see. Perhaps he could do it. He should go and find some puppies as his way of saying thank you for his stay. But he wasn't sure that it would go down too well. He thought he'd look around for Louise and tell her his plan. She'd even know where you could find puppies. But he had to find her first.

He went upstairs to the big landing under the loft where prints of hunting scenes and faded stags on craggy mountains lined the walls. There was a flight of steps hidden away at the end. These led into the huge loft space where he had been trapped once when they had played hide and seek. He'd slammed the trap door down, waited for what seemed hours, then panicked because he hadn't

been found and he couldn't get the door open again. He had broken his nails trying to prize one side up and was just about to scream when Charlie had popped up through the hole and bumped Luke's forehead with the lid. He had had one of those comic type lumps with pain stripes radiating out of its blue sides for the rest of his stay.

There was a strange scratching sound from above. Maybe Louise wasn't in there at all and what he could hear was just mice, or black, plague-bearing, rats. He would trap them and take them to Miss Trant in the church and demand his Tudor penny.

He stretched out his arm and knocked gently on the hatch. The scratching stopped.

'Hello Louise,' he called.

A muffled 'Yes, what do you want?' came back.

'I just wondered where you were. I wanted to ask you something.'

There then came the sound of furniture being dragged across the floor followed by the creaking of the hatch being slowly lifted. She stared down at him, holding a bird's feather which had a glistening blackened tip. She could see him looking at it and quickly put it behind her back. He didn't move. She lowered down the ladder and said, unexpectedly:

'Come up.'

He flopped into the gloomy, musty space lit by a dangling light bulb whose rays fell upon something

big and brown perched on a table. He straightened up and went towards it. He was staring straight into the penetrating glare of a fully grown male buzzard.

Although he felt a bit sick at seeing this stuffed creature so close up he was impressed by its size, its magnificence. The variation of the plumage from brown, cream almost black to black. His upper body was dark to medium brown. The underwing, covert feathers, were downy. He could see how they grew all over the body to protect and control its temperature, they were a dark brown, tawny colour. The chest seemed to be divided from the lower part of the body by a pale brown crescent of very fine feathers.

'What's this doing here?'

'It's Mum's.'

'No, its not anyone's,' he snapped, angry at what he was seeing.

'It's nobody's,' he went on. 'All birds are their own birds just as all men are their own men, if you see what I mean. Are you telling me that Auntie Sue killed this bird and had it stuffed?'

'No, she didn't,' Louise replied indignantly. 'She bought it at an auction years ago.'

Luke collapsed onto an old travelling trunk hidden under the beams.

'Oh, I see.' He calmed down 'I'm sorry,' he added.

'It's great, isn't it? I mean the bird is great, not what

they've done to it.'

Louise agreed: 'This is what the Victorians did, all the time. It was popular.' As she said this she brought the feather she had been holding in her hand into view again. She ran it down the mottled side of the buzzard.

Luke held out his hand towards *Buteo Buteo* and took hold of one of the primaries, trying to fan it out.

'Don't worry, I'm not going to tear the wing off. It's hard to believe that these wings stretch out to 4-5 feet when they lie so compact and smooth here.'

He stroked the buzzard's back and turned to Louise and pointed to the feather in her hand. 'And that? Is that one that's fallen out, and now you don't know just where it's meant to go?'

'No, I found this up the valley and I'm using it as a quill for something I'm working on for Mum. It's to do with what's happening now. I just thought that writing about it, using this real bird's feather would make it more real.'

'Is that a primary or a feather?' He asked, trying to ignore the earnestness in her voice when she had said what's happening now.

'This is a primary, it's whitish and tipped with black, there are about twelve which form the outer part of the wing'

Louise stood twirling the feather in her hand. As she did so he noticed another large object. There was a light coloured piece of wood like an elbow stinking out in the gloom.

'And this…. Wow.. is this yours too…Did you do this?'

He stepped behind her to admire a wooden sculpted version of a buzzard in an angel-stoop position.

'You've got the colours just right,' he gasped.

'I made it from a piece of spelted beech I found in the wood.'

'Cool. It's just right for those different shades of brown, I love it. Now I know what that tapping was about.'

'It's been difficult to keep it quiet I've been working on it when Dad and Charlie are out.'

She added, 'I didn't do the full wing span because it might topple.'

Luke said, 'Common birds have between 1,500 and 3,000 feathers. But these beautiful *Buteo Buteos* don't have so many. You've got them just right,' he ran his hand

over the wood. He eyed up the size of the model. 'This is a female, right, it's larger than the male, larger than this stuffed male. You've got your own pair of buzzards trapped right here.' He grinned.

She looked upset at the word trapped.

'Trapped, that's one of the reasons why our Mum's not here now. It was about the shoot. Well, not the shoot exactly but the preparations leading up to it. They rear these pheasants and partridge out in the woods all over the place and they still think, maybe now thought, that the chicks were being eaten by any bird of prey including buzzards. But there never was and still isn't any evidence. Dad and Riley's Dad were caught up in this. Dad still is, I think. If only he could just break away from Hastercombe and just manage our own animals.'

Luke ran his hand over the soft feathers of the buzzard's sloping shoulder. Louise went on,

'So they poisoned them. They put out poisoned meat for them.'

He didn't like to ask.

'You mean they, Uncle Dan did this, does this?'

'Did, yes. I hope it stays did, now that Radley's Dad is dead, but I'm not sure, but he has stopped maybe because Sugar and Spice when they were around…'

She couldn't go on. There was a pause then Luke ventured.

He hoped that what she was saying didn't mean that

the dogs weren't here because they'd been poisoned by Uncle Dan. No, that couldn't be true.

'Why did he do it?'

'He just had to, he just had to or he would have lost his job,' Louise replied

She went on, 'It was all to do with the shoot. At that time Mr Stacey, the boss at Hastercombe, was making a lot of money from the shoot. It was advertised as the shoot where you could bag the most birds.'

'Great, eh?' said Luke staring into the buzzard's eyes.

'To do that he wanted to make absolutely sure that no birds, rooks, crows, ravens, kestrels, buzzards were destroying the eggs or chicks. So he thought he'd just get rid of them all by poisoning them.'

'Isn't that illegal?'

'Yes, it is, so he decided to set up hoppers legally to poison squirrels with Warfarin. Mum found out that these hoppers didn't contain poisoned grain but dead poisoned squirrel and rabbit flesh so that birds of prey would eat it.'

'And your Dad knew all this?'

'Mum said that he had set them up, but I'm not so sure. I think it was Radley's Dad but, of course, Radley says that that was not true either.'

He flicked through all the photographs and letters on the desk.

'So what are you doing exactly?'

'Well, it's sort of a school project. But really I want

to get it together for Mum so that she can carry on her campaigning against this stuff. I'm a coward too because I would like Dad to see it all and hear what he has to say, but I'm afraid.'

'So you're trying to be a bit of a peacemaker then?' He asked.

'As if. But I thought if I made it look like something that had happened in the past…she couldn't get her thoughts together.

'So that's why you're using the quill and staining these photos brown.'

'Yeah because that way it's more indirect.'

She looked Luke in the eye for approval.

'I wish I knew if he'd really stopped the poisoning and that he will see it as something in the past too.'

At that moment a door banged violently downstairs and there was the sound of frantic footsteps rushing upstairs. Charlie was back.

'Louise, Luke,' he shouted.

'Does Charlie know about this?' Luke whispered to Louise.

'No, not at all, he'd get angry and definitely think I was taking sides against Dad.'

Charlie shouted up the stair well.

'Come on you two, where are you? I've got something to show you.'

Once outside they all three stopped and stared at each other.

'Is it far, shall I take my bike too?' Louise asked

'Er, no better not do that, too much noise,' said Charlie.

Louise and Luke exchanged glances, Luke finding it hard to believe that Charlie didn't want to make a noise for once.

'So we'll walk then yeah?' Luke didn't really ask but just started off in what he thought was going to be the direction.

'No Luke,' Charlie tried to whisper, 'we must go round the back of the house.'

As they slipped down behind Crossways farm a pink hazy line in the sky remained at the bottom of the valley. They were going down towards the mountain bike track in the woods.

'It's a bit late to see anything in the woods isn't it?' Louise asked her brother knowing that wildlife would not be why he was taking them there.

Luke turned to his cousins, 'Badgers, maybe. Do you remember when we all….' He hesitated remembering that things weren't the same for Louise and Luke now without their Mum, but Louise carried on for him.

'Oh yeah, I remember the baby badgers were rolling around and playing in the leaves.'

'And then the badger's Mum came charging out at us and we stumbled away as fast as we could.' Charlie put his finger to his lips and dipped down under the trees by the farm gate where the track met the lane. He gestured to the right.

'I think we're all right now because I don't know exactly where Dad is. Was he in the house?'

'I don't think so,' said Luke. Daylight was fading and the hedges and trees began to break up as they walked along.

'Up here.' He turned into the grassed over lane to the right.

They hesitated before entering, feeling that eyes were watching them as before. A jay chi-chied and flapped away into the top storey of the towering beeches. The walkers were now heading uphill. They came to a crossroads where the lane went bumpily straight. There was another grassed over lane which went to the left. To the right two twisted hornbeam trees formed an arch, their withering seed keys rattling as they pushed through. Charlie plunged under and they followed.

'Wait,' he gestured and took out a billhook from his bag, 'we'll need this.'

The brown of the blade slithered in and out of the brambles at face level as he slashed them down in a backwards movement. They were in a tunnel which had crumbling brown sides topped with livid green moss and overshadowed with elder and hazel branches.

'It's through here.' Charlie said ahead.

They walked haltingly, watching where they trod and keeping back from the bramble slasher. Charlie stopped abruptly and they caught up with him to where he stood

by a break in the hedgerow pointing to a set of steps made from six-inch timber rounds. They were just visible in the gloom climbing upwards. Luke guessed that this must be the hut he had secretly discovered earlier must be at the top, but he said nothing. It was Charlie's discovery now, he wouldn't say that he had come to it from an easier direction close to the MB loop.

'I don't know why I've never seen these steps before, they're not that new. I'm sure no one knows it's here, Dad's not said anything. Has he said anything to you Lou?'

She answered distractedly, 'Er…what…no…where do they go to?'

They came out into the field and there in the dusky, umbered light was a wooden hut. Charlie waited for their cries of surprise. Luke just shifted off and started to walk around the back of the black hut to the concrete platform while the other two squabbled about who knew it was there and what it was for. Luke ran his hand over the grizzly gibbet items he had bumped into before. There was a rustle in the gorse bushes nearby. He didn't want to meet another angry badger and walked around to the front of the hut where Charlie and Louise stood on tiptoe peering through the window.

Louise was saying, 'I went to the gamekeeper's hut once, but it was further into the wood, it must be a ruin by now.'

Charlie ignored his sister's comment and hopped up to

the top step again and felt the edges of the timbers.

'But I don't think these steps are that old, the wood's still rough.'

'Can't see anything inside' said Louise coming down from her tiptoes. Charlie was thrashing around with his billhook again somewhere to the left of the hut.

'Guys, look at these,' he shouted, rummaging under the tarpaulin.

'More timber posts like the ones on the steps'.

They went over to where he stood holding up a green tarpaulin.

'Good for a chicane, d'you think?' Luke suggested.

'Why hasn't Dad said anything about this to us?'

Charlie looked at Louise. 'D'you think we should tell him?'

Luke felt left out of their conspiracy and was still worried by the gibbet at the back, the falling light and the rustling in the gorse. He wasn't feeling such a confident townee now as he said, 'Well, perhaps it's just someone's hideaway and we shouldn't be here really. I thought I heard someone moving about round the back there.'

The screeching of a male tawny owl filled the silence. Luke put his finger to his lips and hooted; a few seconds passed and there it was the response of the female.

'OK guys, it's our secret, yes,' said Charlie

They nodded and descended, almost on tiptoe, back down into the lane and back to Crossways in silence.

8 SLAMMING ON THE BINDERS

The next morning Mr Brooking asked cheerily, 'What are you all up to today?'

'Just riding around a bit,' replied Luke.

'Still got course work to do,' added Louise.

Charlie said, 'Don't know.'

Mr Brooking asked with a smile, 'Would you like to come into town with me in the Land Rover?'

There was a pause, his children didn't respond immediately, even though he knew that Luke would jump at a chance to ride in the Land Rover.

'Oh, come on you two, you can go out on the bikes later. And that course work can wait Lou, you deserve a break,' coaxed Mr Brooking. Luke gave her a sideways look knowing what he did about the buzzard sculpture and said, 'Yes I'll come, I'll just go and get my money, I'd like to check out your bike shop again anyway.'

Louise shrugged her shoulders and said, 'OK Dad.'

'Lunch in McDonald's,' Mr Brooking added to get his

son on board.

'Oh alright then, cool.' Charlie was on his way to the door.

* * *

After Mr Brooking left them to do some business they wandered down the narrow High Street of the little market town. Charlie said, 'D'you think those fence posts are there ready to fence us off from getting into our MX wood? Who would want to do that?'

Louise looked as if she was about to answer but turned abruptly to look into a shop window full of the coming summer fashions.

'See you later guys,' she said watching them carry on down the street.

'Fencing, yeh I suppose you might be right, it can't be anything to do with our farm, though because it would be waiting in our yard,' said Charlie.

'Might have been delivered where the job was going to be,' Luke suggested.

'No, Dad always keeps his deliveries close to home to start with, things go missing otherwise, you know.'

They had come to a halt outside a sports shop window which had a poster advertising:

> **FALCONRY DISPLAY**
> **FAIRSTONE MANOR**
> **10am**

'That's tomorrow,' said Luke.

'Fairstone Manor, is that near here?' Luke asked Charlie. Maybe he could fit it in before he left for London.

'About five miles. No, maybe less.'

'I could cycle there, what about you? D'you want to go too?'

'Well, it depends what's happening around the club, whether they'll let me out with them again,' Charlie replied.

'OK. I suppose I could go and still get back in time for my train home. Suppose so,' said Luke, not really interested in going to see birds on poles anyway. He preferred to see them flying freely when they wanted to.

Outside it had started to rain and a wind was whipping up through the bright green lime leaves on the trees at the edge of the pavement.

'As Luke's here why don't we take him along to the new climbing wall at the Sports Centre or the swimming pool, or crazy golf?'

The climbing wall at the Sports Centre sounded like a good idea.

Charlie didn't look too happy and Louise was slightly puzzled by the fact that her Dad didn't want to get straight back to the farm as he normally did.

'Well, OK, I suppose I could have a look at the climbing wall.'

'A climbing wall,' Luke smiled at the idea, 'we've got

one at home,' he said. 'But it seems strange to have one here when Dartmoor is so close. Why not just go and climb up the tors?'

'Well, you've got to start somewhere,' said Mr Brooking in its defence. 'It's good practice.'

So they all went off to the Sports Centre for the morning.

When they'd all had their fill of fish and chips (they'd not made it to McDonald's as they'd passed the chippy first), Mr Brooking led them back to the truck for another surprise. He pulled back a familiar looking tarpaulin at the back of the truck.

'I've brought your bikes, yes, and yours Louise, because here's another kind of course I want you all to see.'

He held his fingers up in the shape of a cross on its side and then made a curved C with his thumb and forefinger. This was the old mad Dad making a come-back alright.

As they sped through the town Louise just caught a glimpse of Radley, hunched up in his hoodie sitting in a corner café with two rough looking teenagers who were listening to every word he said. Yes, yes, yes she screamed to herself.

Mr Brooking started to steer the truck out into open country once they were out of the town.

'Right, me 'andsome riders', he said, tapping on the steering wheel to get their attention.

'You've ridden BMXs.'

'Please Dad,' groaned Charlie.

'Mountain bikes, Moto-Cross bikes and Enduros too. You've ridden courses made for all of them. But what about something bigger, more challenging?'

They didn't respond so he went on, 'We're going to go for a cross country course, an XC, and I'm coming with you.'

They remained silent.

'I'm going to hire a bike when I get there.'

And that's what he did. They all set off on a 12-mile circuit. It was a tight single track running by the side of ploughed fields and through woodlands. Some hills took them up to a hundred and fifty metres in places. Luke didn't think that his Uncle would make it sometimes. Still not sure what to make of his possible 'poisoning' activities that Louise had told him about, he shouted out instructions to help him along at certain points on the route.

'Keep your elbows out a bit more Uncle Dan, in an attack position.'

'Angel-Stoop,' Louise added.

'Keep shifting your weight. Move your chest round the corners, not just your arms. They pushed hard up a flock-flack route through the woods. Luke thought of Jack's twenty-niner wheels and how they would bring him up here quicker.

Once into the conifer wood Louise took the lead

looking out for white arrows painted on the trees to show the way. They came to a glade and Louise, Luke and Uncle Dan were thrilled to catch the glimpse of a buzzard rolling over and locking talons with a raven. They were fighting over whose nesting area this was soon to be.

Charlie, now stuck in after a reluctant start, shouted to his Dad as they went for the freeride, 'Put your brakes on Dad, use your outside foot, get your front wheel into the ruts.'

Luke added, 'Use the trail edge, Uncle Dan, not your brakes all the time.'

They all finished the route more or less at the same time, although Charlie, because of the neglected state of his bike, lagged behind a bit.

Uncle Dan stood looking proud. 'Well, you certainly know what you're talking about – it's hard work, isn't it? What did you think of travelling through the countryside like that?'

'It'd be quicker on my Moto-Cross bike and it wasn't muddy enough,' Charlie moaned.

'I loved it and I didn't have to worry about step-ups and step-downs and all that fancy stuff,' said Louise.

'You sound like one of the old-style Daleks before they learnt how to levitate.' Luke said and went on, 'Great Uncle Dan to be out in the country all the time. We can't do that where I live. Those single track bits give you time to look around – what great countryside.'

'For birds too,' his uncle added.

'You've heard of horses for courses. Well, there are bikes for trails too.'

Even after all this it seemed that they weren't going to go home yet and Charlie was beginning to feel a bit hard done by – had he missed an opportunity to go out night riding or not? Only the answerphone could tell him that when they got back. Louise didn't seem too worried about her course work for a change and just agreed with everything that her Dad suggested. She kept glancing sideways at him as they drove along as if he was about to give a sign for action soon, and that she would have to follow this. It was puzzling. His Uncle Dan was Uncle Dan again. So what did he want to do with them now.

'Mr Gregory told me that his barn owls are still here. The barn owls are out hunting in the evening dimpsey. I expect Luke would like to go and see them, then we'll do

a loop round back home to the village. The fish and chip van comes tonight. Twice in one day for fish and chips, why not. You've got your binoculars with you haven't you Luke?'

Mr Brooking reached into the storage shelf under the steering wheel. 'Yours should be here Charlie too, you can share them with Lou.'

This was strange behaviour. It seems that Dan

Brooking wanted to stay away from Crossways for as long as he could. And now he was encouraging an interest in birdwatching when he had made such a fuss about his wife buying a telescope and tripod a few months ago. No wonder that she took it with her when she left. Charlie and his Mum had enjoyed watching the stars through it. Charlie thought that if he did go out with the club at night he would be able to tell them where they were if they got lost because he knew the position of the plough and some planets sitting low in the sky at this time of year.

They pulled up in Mr Gregory's farmyard and were greeted by the excited yapping of his collie dogs. One had only got three legs but he ran the fastest and was always in front of the others. There she was covering Louise in licks as she got out. How they all missed Sugar and Spice.

'Good evening Dan and family,' Mr Gregory said.

'Hello, Harry,' said Mr Brooking. 'Remember Luke, our town cousin.'

Mr Gregory stood back and gave Luke a hard stare.

'Of course,' said Mr Gregory. 'I think you know more about birds than we country folk who just take them for granted. I found your bike in the woods last time didn't I? You'd been out looking for woodpeckers, you told me, and that you had heard a cuckoo and wandered off down to the lake and couldn't find your way back.'

'I'm sorry, Mr Gregory.'

'Don't worry. It was a good job I found your bike – you

never know now with those trial riders about.'

Charlie looked away and fiddled with the strap on the binoculars. Mr Gregory started walking and whispered over his shoulder, 'Follow me.'

They all walked off round the back of the jumble of buildings which ran down from the yard. He led them down an alley between two of the outhouses, halted suddenly and put a finger to his lips. He pointed to where the edge of the open building met the sky. Charlie noticed that the dog star, old Cirus, was out already and he thought of the telescope and his Mum again. He wished he hadn't been so difficult sometimes when they were out on the river and she'd told him to be still then the kingfishers would come. He'd just splashed about and thrown stones across to the far bank destroying any chance of this.

A white and gold silent bird drifted out and across to the edge of the copse. There he goes, they all thought, and Luke wondered how long they would have to wait before he returned. There would be competition from the buzzards who could be circling around everywhere now away from their home territories. After all they could spot their prey from a mile up and in nature it was always first come, first served.

9 ROARING RISERS

'This is a message for Luke Brooking from the Traillee Raiders.

Meet at Hastercombe Gates at Midnight tonight for…' there was a pause and then an echo-like voice came down the phone, 'a r-i-d-e into the d-a-r-k', cackling laughter followed. Then back to normal with a short sharp, ring Big Bog on 846231 to confirm, cheers.'

They were all standing in the living-room as the answer phone message played back. Louise slapped her brother on the shoulder and, of course, that set him off pogoing and whooping about the room in his own noisy way. She laughed, 'Are you up to a r-i-d-e into the d-a-r-k.'

Now he was punching the air and leaping over the sofa. For a second he thought of how Sugar and Spice would have joined in with their whines and yaps.

'Great Charlie, I wish I could be here to see you, well hear you anyway. Probably will, Hastercombe's not far away.'

Mr Brooking said, in a bit of a grumpy voice, 'They're up to anything to bring people in, and get their money. Calm down Charlie, you're not going anyway. No roistering about in the dark for you.'

'I've got good lights, so has Luke,' Charlie quickly intervened.

'No, Charlie, it's late. I'll take you both over to walk the course first thing, if you want, or take the bikes,' his Dad said.

Charlie ran out of the room into the yard. He was gone with his Dad not far behind.

'Poor old Charlie and his traillee obsession,' said Luke to Louise.

'Yes, you said he was hanging around the other day when you checked out the loop. He wants to run with the hare and shoot with the hounds.'

'He knows his birds too.' although he pretends he doesn't,' added Luke.

At the mention of the B word Louise bid them goodnight and set off upstairs. Luke heard her footsteps creaking up the narrow stairs which led to the attic and her model. He went straight to bed, the sound of the owls calling lulled him to sleep. It was much nicer to listen to them here than at home because there he had to go out into the alley which ran along the back of his house and stand in the cold for hours. Here he lay cosy and warm in bed and they just serenaded him to sleep.

* * *

But what was this? A vision of smelly trainers waving under his nose shocked him awake. He pushed them aside and sat up. There was Charlie bent double by his bedside with his fingers to his lips telling him to be quiet.

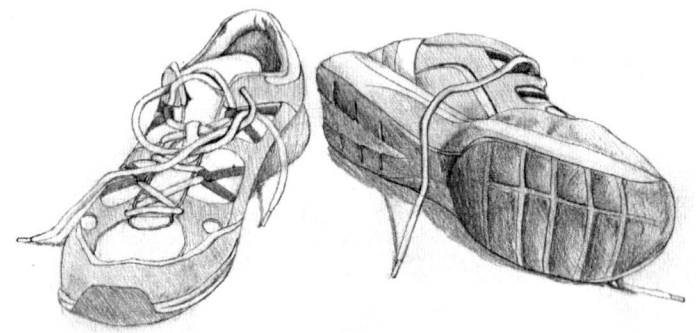

'Sh, come on, wake up. Come with me. I've got the bikes ready, we're going to Hastercombe to check out the night ride route. You won't be here on Sunday and I'd like you to see it. I can't take the trail bike, Dad will hear me.'

Luke rubbed his eyes, 'Aren't we going with your Dad tomorrow?'

'That's what he says but he's really too busy round the farm and with the lambing.'

'Isn't he out there now doing that, won't he see us.'

'No Luke, I've checked, he's just come in.'

He waved the trainers under his nose again, but Luke pushed them away and pulled the duvet up around his ears.

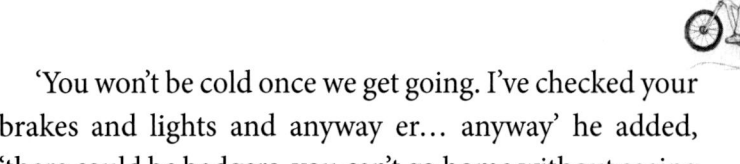

'You won't be cold once we get going. I've checked your brakes and lights and anyway er… anyway' he added, 'there could be badgers, you can't go home without seeing them again, can you?'

Charlie was now keen to get out on two counts. He'd just checked Luke's lights. And what lights! He'd got a Lupine Lighting System called, Nightmare Li-ion Pro, which charged from the wheels. Charlie's clip-on battery lamp for his bike would just have to do for now.

'Badgers,' Luke whispered rather loudly and sat up ready for the off. He whinced a bit as his muscles were still aching from the climbing wall and the cross country course, but badgers, yes. He pulled his clothes on over his pyjamas.

Charlie asked, 'How long do your lights burn for then?'

'One and a half hours full on, and nearly three, low. But my lights are nothing to the barn owl's kind of sonic vision.'

As he dressed he realized there was another sound outside now, not the calling of owls – it was raining. Still, a good chance to put on his Laser jacket Mum had bought for him just before he left. She reminded him that it did rain a lot in Devon and he'd been lucky so far. This one was so cool, it folded up into its own pocket. He struggled to shake it out and felt envious of Nickwing and all the other birds out there in the wet who only had to shake their feathers to keep dry.

They pedalled along in the streaming dark with the odd bat veering away from them as they went. The roads were damp but it wasn't raining heavily and Luke sprung awake to the adventure with the promise of badgers somewhere along the route.

By the wood Charlie gestured to Luke to focus his beam between two posts where the route began. Rain streamed across the spotlight. There was a flat area which seemed to drop away.

They waited for what seemed like ages for any sign of the bike lights flickering towards them, but none came. They heard a lorry pass by on the top road, but didn't see any lights. Was it a ghost American lorry from the time when this area was occupied in the Second World War? Was that why it had no lights?

'Let's go down to the gates, they said they were meeting there, hope we're not too late.'

They hauled on their bars and turned back down to the gates and the meadow below where sheep grazed safely most of the time. They sped along the lane in a tunnel made by the overhanging branches. When these weren't overhead and the rain clouds came through it was as if they were up there themselves helping to tip it down. Suddenly they were out by the open meadow, they slammed on the binders.

'Cut the lights,' whispered Charlie. The young men in front of them carrying torches were too busy pushing

sheep up into the back of a lorry to notice them anyway. Charlie whipped out his mobile phone, he knew his Dad would be alert, not fully asleep at this time of year. He whispered his info into the glowing face of the black plastic slab as soon as his Dad answered. He didn't give him any time to moan about what he was doing out there in the middle of the night anyway.

'What shall we do now?' asked Luke.

'We might as well wait until the police get here,' said Charlie.

But then it happened. Barreling down from the opposite side of the road came ten thundering, thumping,

mud spattered headlights of the trial bikers all standing up on their pegs and hollering.

There was the sound of whirring wheels and Charlie and Luke were caught in the lights of a group of MB riders doing their own night ride and standing up on their pedals shouting and waving at the rustlers too. This sudden noise and light sent the sheep scattering off from inside the lorry and out over the fields looking for a leader to follow. Charlie knew what to do. He'd watched his Dad and helped him often enough. Luke moved fast too.

The rustlers were left stranded on the tail gate like frightened chickens shielding their eyes from the motocross headlights.

Luke shouted out to the MB riders, 'Drop your bikes quick follow me.'

They raised the lorry's tail gate sending the rustlers tumbling back into their own jail. Cheers went up on all sides. From over in the direction of the farm came the sirens wailing, lights flick-flacked through the woods – the police were on their way.

10 ALL GO FOR GREEN

Saturday morning dawned clear, crisp and bright. The dew soon evaporated from the meadows and hung in wispy clouds in the tree-tops so that the buzzards were forced to scoop under them and swoop low along the hedgerows on their first hunting forays.

Toc! Toc! Toc! The last post was in.

'There, it's done. Thanks a lot. All we need now is the information boards, well done,' he said.

'Will there be a sign before they get here though?' she asked.

'I'll make sure there is, don't worry about that, it'll be there.'

'Shall I help?' she asked.

Radley popped up from nowhere and replied immediately, 'Don't worry. I'll go up into the woods in a minute.' He rummaged around amongst the loose bits of timber lying on the platform. 'I'll paint an arrow on this board like it's a diversion and then they're sure to come down.'

'Oh,' the boy said quietly, stuffing his hands into his hoodie pockets and pushing his ginger hair back over his forehead.

The woman looked at him suspiciously and then said, 'I wonder if those two are up and about yet.'

She looked at Dan, 'I hear they had a bit of a busy night.

'It certainly was, he replied.

'I'll go and bring them over. See you soon.'

Radley could not get away quick enough when he saw Mr and Mrs Brooking standing together, holding hands, on the viewing platform.

* * *

'Had a good week Luke?' Mr Brooking asked as they chugged along. Despite his protests Uncle Dan had insisted on driving him to the station to catch his train back to London. The bike was securely fastened onto the back of the family car with a new clip-on, high snap-on bike rack.

'Oh yes, thank you Uncle Dan, it's been great, full of surprises,' he replied sleepily, still tired after last night's events. But he still had really wanted to ride to the station.

'But I'd really like to ride to the station one last time, can you let me down here. It'll be my last ride through the countryside, please Uncle Dan.'

'OK. I'll drop you off here.'

Luke felt like speeding around for a bit so, before heading straight for the wood he did a few laps of honour

up and down the straight section of the road to get rid of his anger about having to go home with so many things left unexplained. Now here was Nickwing gyrating above him and scooping down out of sight below the tree line.

Luke began the long steep climb up to the top of the circuit. He could hear some dogs barking excitedly off to the left. Their yaps were coming nearer – he started to pedal faster feeling a bit worried about their approach. But they didn't sound aggressive, just full of beans. He dropped down into the slalom single track and could see at the bottom something which had not been there a few days ago. It was a chicane made out of brand new fence posts.

He flick-flacked through with ease and was into the whoops when out of a gap in the hedge burst two lolloping long-haired, sandy-coloured retrievers intent on catching up with him. No, it couldn't be!

He shouted out, 'Sugar, Spice. Slow Down.'

And there standing by the gap in the hedge was his Uncle Dan hand in hand with…no, this couldn't be true either. His Auntie Sue. She came towards him and put her arm around his shoulder.

'Hello, Luke, I hope we didn't frighten you too much.'

She bent down to the dogs, 'Calm down you two. Look how they remember you. Don't look so startled.' She looked up at Luke.

'You remember me too don't you?'

'Yes, of course, Auntie Sue.'

He gave his Uncle Dan a puzzled look. 'How are you? And the dogs are OK too.'

'Fine. We're all fine, just been away for a bit. Now for another surprise.'

Luke followed them through the gap in the hedge, Sugar and Spice still jumping up to nuzzle him. They were obviously so glad to be home and broke off to plunge themselves into patches of stinking billy which lined the track. They passed the outline of the old Keeper's Cottage and the head-high stingy nettles which waved a warning to any who ventured off in that direction. But someone must have risked it. Here was Radley's diversion sign. Sugar and Spice held their noses high to take the scent and plunged in.

Now that they had stopped barking there came the thump, thump of a trial bike. It was getting nearer and nearer. Here came Charlie bursting through from nowhere on his MX, his leggings covered in mud. He wanted to say goodbye to Luke and ride alongside him somehow to the station, but he had heard familiar barks and been diverted. His bike stalled as the dogs knocked him flying. This time it was the sight of his Mum and Dad standing there, holding hands, which mired him in the gloop. His Mum ran over and helped him up; he got a big hug too. They all stood around the outside of the hut on the viewing platform which had seats and a table at the

end raised up on a pile of rocks. Uncle Dan, Auntie Sue, Charlie, Sugar and Spice. It was inevitable that Radley should pop up too this time from the side of the hut. He came wheeling Charlie's old MB. It had been cleaned up and wasn't looking too bad. Charlie stepped forward and was about to ask what was going on when from around the other side of the shed Luke's Mum appeared, she was wheeling his old MB from London.

'What's going on?' chorused Charlie and Luke.

'Let me explain,' said Mr Brooking, stepping forward and taking his wife's hand.

'Sue's been away and now she's back. I've been away somewhere else to, doing things I wasn't sure about, and I won't do again.'

Mrs Brooking stepped forward, 'I went away because of this, but I wanted to find a way to come back and change things.'

She turned to Charlie. 'Remember your old Uncle Fred?' Charlie nodded.

'Well, because he can't ride his bike any more he wanted to find out ways he could help cyclists.'

'Just cyclists?' Charlie questioned.

'Oh no, he is interested in anybody who loves two wheels and the open air. So he helped us out, me and your Dad. We've bought the land and farmhouse now and so are separate from the Hastercombe Estate's corporate ways. But Uncle Fred gave us the money on the proviso

that we set up something for all two-wheelers. And here it is.' She turned around on the platform.

'From now on we'll work this land as it should be worked. They'll be no more poisoning of birds or any other animals,' said Uncle Dan.

Luke's Mum spoke up, 'We townees don't know what's going on a lot of the time and make such a fuss about 'motors' whizzing about in what we think should be a quiet and peaceful countryside.'

'People have to work with machines – and have fun too so there will always be some noise about,' chipped in Radley.

That boy again, thought Luke, always running with the hare and shooting with the hounds.

The door of the hut creaked open and out came Louise cradling the beautiful carved sculpture of *Buteo Buteo* in his Angle-Stoop position. Auntie Sue's eyes widened. Louise said, 'Live and let live.'

Mr Brooking said, 'Well, that's exactly what we can do now. We'll have two trails, the MB and the traillee. But they're not going to do their runs at the same time and some things for the traillees will be completely different – longer loops for a start. This hut is now the office for making bookings to use our new trails.'

Louise added, 'We've got a time-table for everyone to come and do repairs along the track and build new whoops and chicanes. Everyone, even Radley here who incidently makes a great spy, without him setting up the Night Ride and bringing in the rustlers when he did yesterday we'd have no sheep to manage on OUR farm now.'

Charlie stepped up: 'But what's he doing with my old MB bike?'

'Well,' his Mum said, 'because he was so helpful in capturing the rustlers and helping out with the trail set up… We're giving him your old bike.'

Charlie looked straight at Radley, 'It was you, wasn't it? You were the one who phoned and said come for a ride into the dark, it wasn't the club at all.'

'No sorry Charlie,' Radley said. 'But you did get to see them in action, didn't you. And they are on our side, they want to keep farmers happy too.'

Now Luke's Mum stepped forward to come between Charlie and Radley.

'I've brought your old MB down Luke to give to Charlie. Uncle Dan said, that after yesterday's XC he seemed keen to still keep using muscle-powered two-wheelers but that he needed a bike with a bit more power.'

Charlie moved over to the bike, tested the shockies, looked down at the Deralleur gears and the Shimano break system. He grinned up at them, 'Thanks, it looks like this might need a bit of tuning though.'

Louise moaned as the boys were back again using their techy terms.

'This place is great Dad.'

Radley, full of confidence now said, 'I nailed those claws and stuff to the back of the door from the old gamekeeper's hut to remind us of how it used to be.'

Mr Brooking put his arm around Charlie's shoulders, 'Creatures being persecuted for the wrong reasons, we've got to be sure that doesn't happen again. The thing you have to remember about Moto-Cross Charlie is that…'

As his son broke free from what sounded like the beginning of one of those complicated grown-up discussions which come to no conclusion whatsoever everything was interrupted by a piercing: 'Pee-yo-wow!' directly above their heads.

Nickwing caterpulted into the blue above them. He turned and dropped gently down into the crown of the Monterey Pine which would always be there for him, and the bikers, in the years to come.